This book is for Jasmine.

**Jas, we wrote you this book because
we love playing this game with you.**

Love, your godparents

Little, Brown and Company

New York   Boston

**The illustrations for this book were drawn and colored
digitally. The text was set in Sentinel.**

Hello!

Let's read this book together.

But first, I just need to check a few things.

Is this a triangle?

Is this a cat?

And what's this?

Excellent!

Great job.

It's good to know we agree.

Let's get started.

This is a ball.

Are you sure?
Hmmm ...
I think you need to look closer.

This is a dog.

Nah, it's a dog for sure.
I can see its eye. Its legs. It must be a dog.

This is a bike.

**Look at the wheels.
It's definitely a bike.**

This is a blue bike.

You think it's yellow?
No way!
It's blue.
Like a tomato.

This is a
happy princess.

Of course it's a princess!
I can see her big smile.

This is a
scary monster.

What do you mean?
You think <u>this</u> is the princess?
I think you're a bit confused.

This is a monster scaring a princess.

You are getting very mixed up.

This is a monster
scaring a princess
and her pet dog.

We talked about this before.
Don't you remember?
Look at its tail!
All dogs have tails.

This is a beach.

What do you mean it's <u>not</u> a beach?
I can see the sky.
And the ground . . .

This is a kite.

It has to be a kite.
Why else would it have a long string?

This is a princess flying a kite at the beach.

Are you feeling okay?
You seem to be getting
a lot of things wrong today.

This is a princess flying a kite at the beach with her pet dog.

Are your eyes working properly?
We might need to take your temperature.

This is a monster telling a story about a princess flying her kite at the beach with her pet dog.

This is getting silly.

This is a monster telling a story about a princess flying her kite at the beach with her pet dog, while standing on a block.

It can't be a ball.
Look at the cover of this book.
See? That's a ball.

**This is not
the end
of the book.**